THIS BOOK
BELONGS TO:

ALL RIGHTS RESERVED.
PUBLISHED IN THE UNITED STATES BY CLARKSON POTTER/PUBLISHERS,
AN IMPRINT OF THE CROWN PUBLISHING GROUP, A DIVISION OF
PENGUIN RANDOM HOUSE LLC, NEW YORK.
CROWNPUBLISHING.COM
CLARKSONPOTTER.COM

CLARKSON POTTER IS A TRADEMARK AND POTTER WITH COLOPHON
IS A REGISTERED TRADEMARK OF PENGUIN RANDOM HOUSE LLC.

ISBN 978-1-9848-2424-0

PRINTED IN THE UNITED STATES OF AMERICA
TEXT BY SAMANTHA LEWIS
BOOK DESIGN BY NICOLE BLOCK
COVER DESIGN BY DANIELLE DESCHENES AND NICOLE BLOCK

10 9 8 7 6 5 4 3 2 1
FIRST EDITION

CAPTAIN MARVEL'S SYMBOL IS A BIG PART OF HER IDENTITY.
DRAW A SYMBOL OF YOUR OWN TO IDENTIFY
WHO YOU ARE TO OTHERS.

JANUARY

2

WHAT SONG MAKES YOU FEEL CONFIDENT?
WRITE ABOUT IT HERE.

THE AVENGERS, THE GUARDIANS OF THE GALAXY,
AND MANY OTHERS ARE FIGHTING FOR JUSTICE
AND PROTECTING OUR WORLD.
WHAT ORGANIZATIONS OR PEOPLE DO YOU KNOW
THAT ARE MAKING THE WORLD A BETTER PLACE?

JANUARY

4

**WHO IN YOUR LIFE GIVES
THE BEST ADVICE
AND WHY?**

HAS THERE BEEN A TIME IN YOUR LIFE
WHEN YOU NEEDED TO BE COURAGEOUS?
WHAT WAS THE SITUATION AND WHAT DID YOU DO?

JANUARY

5

CHOOSE THREE WORDS THAT YOU THINK THE PEOPLE
CLOSEST TO YOU WOULD USE TO DESCRIBE YOU.
**DID YOU AUTOMATICALLY GO FOR POSITIVE
OR NEGATIVE WORDS?**

IT TAKES COURAGE TO ADMIT WHEN YOU DISAGREE WITH
SOMEBODY. WHEN WAS THE LAST TIME YOU HAD
A DIFFERENT OPINION THAN SOMEONE ELSE?
DID YOU SHARE IT?

7

JANUARY

8

**DO YOU WORRY ABOUT WHAT
OTHER PEOPLE THINK?
WHAT ARE SOME WAYS YOU CAN PAY
LESS ATTENTION TO THOSE OPINIONS?**

**WRITE ABOUT A TIME YOU SAW
SOMEONE DO SOMETHING BRAVE.
WHAT DID YOU LEARN?**

JANUARY

9

JANUARY

10

"Things you don't expect come up, and you have to adapt. You can't let it throw you off. You have to cope. Those are all really valuable skills, in life and racing."

MIKAELA SHIFFRIN, OLYMPIC SKIER

SOMETIMES THINGS DON'T GO ACCORDING TO PLAN. HOW DO YOU PERSEVERE IN THESE MOMENTS?

FINISH THIS SENTENCE:
"I BELIEVE THAT I CAN _____ ."

JANUARY

11

JANUARY

12

AS FAST AS YOU CAN, WRITE DOWN TEN THINGS THAT YOU'RE MOST PROUD OF IN EACH OF THE NUMBERED SLOTS BELOW.

 1

 6

 3

 7

 3

 8

 4

 9

 5

 10

WRITE ABOUT A TIME YOU DID SOMETHING YOU WERE AFRAID TO TRY.

13

14

WHAT DO YOU DO WHEN YOU WANT
TO FEEL MORE CONFIDENT?

THINK ABOUT A TIME WHEN YOU STRUGGLED WITH SOMETHING NEW. HOW DID YOU OVERCOME THAT THING?

JANUARY

15

JANUARY

16

NOT ALL SUPER HEROES WEAR CAPES.
MAKE A LIST OF THE PEOPLE IN YOUR LIFE
WHO ARE EVERYDAY SUPER HEROES.

**WHAT IS YOUR BIGGEST GOAL?
HOW CAN YOU OVERCOME THE OBSTACLES
IN YOUR WAY THAT ARE KEEPING YOU
FROM ACHIEVING IT?**

JANUARY

18

IF YOU COULD INVENT ONE THING THAT WOULD HELP SOMEONE ELSE, WHAT WOULD IT BE . . . AND WHY?

**WRITE ABOUT A PERSON YOU ADMIRE.
WHAT QUALITIES DO YOU HAVE
IN COMMON WITH THEM?**

WRITE ABOUT A TIME WHEN YOU HELPED SOMEONE ELSE.
WHAT DID YOU DO AND HOW DID IT MAKE YOU FEEL?

"Returning violence for violence multiplies violence, adding deeper darkness to a night already devoid of stars. Darkness cannot drive out darkness: only light can do that."

———

MARTIN LUTHER KING JR., CIVIL RIGHTS ACTIVIST

AROUND THIS TIME WE CELEBRATE THE LIFE AND WORK OF MARTIN LUTHER KING JR.
HOW WILL YOU ADVOCATE FOR PEACE TODAY?

WHAT MAKES A SUPER HERO
SUPER?

**DESCRIBE AN AREA OF YOUR LIFE THAT
YOU WISH YOU WERE BRAVER IN.
WHAT IS IT AND WHAT'S HOLDING YOU BACK?**

JANUARY

23

JANUARY

24

WHAT IS YOUR FAVORITE POWER POSE? DRAW YOURSELF MAKING IT HERE.

**CAPTAIN MARVEL'S CATCHPHRASE IS
"HIGHER, FURTHER, FASTER."
WHAT WOULD YOUR CATCHPHRASE BE?**

25

26

WRITE ABOUT A MEMBER OF YOUR FAMILY WHO INSPIRES YOU.

WHAT MAKES YOU FEEL STRONG OR INVINCIBLE?

JANUARY

28

**LIST FIVE THINGS YOU LIKE ABOUT YOURSELF.
THEY CAN BE QUALITIES, SKILLS, OR SOME PART OF YOUR
PERSONALITY THAT MAKES YOU FEEL GOOD.**

1

2

3

4

5

**THROUGHOUT HISTORY, THERE HAVE BEEN A LOT OF WOMEN LIKE CAPTAIN MARVEL WHO HAVE MADE THE WORLD A BETTER PLACE.
LIST FIVE WOMEN WHO HAVE SUCCEEDED IN MAKING A DIFFERENCE AND CHOOSE ONE THAT YOU'D LIKE TO LEARN MORE ABOUT.**

JANUARY
29

JANUARY

30

AS CAPTAIN MARVEL LEARNS THE TRUTH OF HER PAST,
SHE HAS TO REVISIT HER OWN IDENTITY.
WHAT MOMENTS, EVENTS, OR PEOPLE IN YOUR PAST
HELPED DEFINE WHO YOU ARE?

WHEN WAS THE LAST TIME SOMEONE TOLD YOU
NOT TO DO SOMETHING YOU WANTED TO DO?
DID IT STOP YOU?

FEBRUARY

1

MANY PEOPLE HAVE UNDERESTIMATED
CAPTAIN MARVEL BECAUSE SHE'S A WOMAN.
HAS ANYONE EVER BEEN BIASED TOWARD YOU
BECAUSE OF YOUR GENDER? HOW DID YOU REACT?

CAPTAIN MARVEL IS ALWAYS WATCHING OUT FOR NICK FURY. WHICH OF YOUR FRIENDS IS THERE FOR YOU NO MATTER WHAT?

FEBRUARY

3

WHEN WAS THE LAST TIME YOU WERE
IMPRESSED WITH YOURSELF?

"All adventures, especially into
new territory, are scary."

SALLY RIDE, ASTRONAUT

WRITE ABOUT A TIME YOU TRIED
SOMETHING THAT SCARED YOU.

5

**DRAW A PICTURE OF YOURSELF SAVING THE CITY
WITH YOUR FAVORITE SUPER HERO.**

**WRITE ABOUT A FAMILY TRADITION THAT
IS A BIG PART OF YOUR IDENTITY.
WHY IS IT IMPORTANT TO YOU?**

1

IF YOU HAD
SUPER HERO POWERS,
WHAT WOULD THEY BE?

CAPTAIN MARVEL DOESN'T ALWAYS FEEL LIKE SHE FITS IN WITH THE OTHER KREE STARFORCE MEMBERS. WHEN WAS THE LAST TIME YOU FELT LIKE AN OUTSIDER?

FEBRUARY

8

FEBRUARY

9

WRITE ABOUT ONE THING
THAT SCARES YOU.

WRITE A SHORT SPEECH OR PEP TALK TO GIVE YOURSELF
THE NEXT TIME YOU FEEL SAD OR DOWN.
WHAT WILL YOU MAKE YOUR SPEECH ABOUT?

FEBRUARY

FINISH THIS SENTENCE:
"I AM IMPORTANT BECAUSE _____ ."

11

WRITE ABOUT A TIME YOU HAD TO MAKE A TOUGH DECISION
THAT WAS ULTIMATELY THE RIGHT CHOICE.
WHAT DID YOU LEARN?

FEBRUARY

13

WHAT
UNIQUE QUALITY
MAKES YOU SPECIAL?

TODAY IS VALENTINE'S DAY.
WRITE A LETTER TO SOMEONE YOU LOVE
ABOUT THEIR BEST QUALITY.

HAPPY
VALENTINE'S
DAY!

FEBRUARY

15

WHEN THE KREE MEMBERS OF THE STARFORCE PREPARE FOR BATTLE, THEIR UNIFORMS CHANGE COLOR. WHAT COLOR MAKES YOU FEEL STRONG AND WHY?

HAVE YOU EVER NOTICED SOMEONE BEING LEFT OUT OR EXCLUDED? DID YOU HELP THEM?

16

FEBRUARY

17

WHAT ARTICLE OF CLOTHING OR OUTFIT HAVE YOU NEVER
HAD THE GUTS TO WEAR?
WEAR IT TODAY AND WRITE ABOUT
THE EXPERIENCE HERE.

**CAPTAIN MARVEL IS ONE OF THE STRONGEST
AVENGERS OUT THERE.
WHAT SPORT, SUBJECT, OR ACTIVITY
ARE YOU STRONGEST IN?**

18

FINISH THIS SENTENCE:
"EVERY DAY, I SHOW COURAGE BY _____ ."

WE ALL MAKE CHOICES WE REGRET, EVEN OUR HEROES.
WHAT IS SOMETHING YOU REGRET,
AND HOW DID YOU LEARN FROM IT?

FEBRUARY

21

ENCOURAGE SOMEONE TO BE BRAVE TODAY.
WRITE A HAIKU ABOUT YOUR EXPERIENCE.

YOU'VE BEEN ASKED TO PUT TOGETHER THE STRONGEST
TEAM TO SAVE THE UNIVERSE.
WHO WOULD YOU CHOOSE AND HOW WILL THEY HELP YOU?

FEBRUARY

23

CAPTAIN MARVEL SOMETIMES HAS TO BREAK
THE RULES IN ORDER TO DO THE RIGHT THING.
HAVE YOU EVER HAD TO BREAK A RULE TO HELP SOMEONE?

WHAT DOES
"FEELING EMPOWERED"
MEAN TO YOU?

**HOW DO YOU FEEL WHEN YOU SEE
STRONG FEMALE CHARACTERS LIKE CAPTAIN MARVEL
IN BOOKS, TV SHOWS, AND MOVIES?**

**CAPTAIN MARVEL STAYS STRONG BY BOXING
WITH HER STARFORCE TEAMMATES.
WHAT IS YOUR FAVORITE SPORT
OR WAY OF BEING ACTIVE?**

26

FEBRUARY

27

"Promise me you'll always remember:
You're braver than you believe, and stronger
than you seem, and smarter than you think."

*POOH'S GRAND ADVENTURE:
THE SEARCH FOR CHRISTOPHER ROBIN*

WRITE ABOUT A TIME YOU USED YOUR DETERMINATION TO ACHIEVE A GOAL.

CAPTAIN MARVEL TRAVELS TO EARTH DURING THE 1990S, WHEN CELL PHONES AND SOCIAL MEDIA DIDN'T EXIST YET. TRY TO GO A FULL DAY WITHOUT USING SOCIAL MEDIA. WERE YOU SUCCESSFUL?

FEBRUARY

28

29

LEAP DAYS HAPPEN ONCE EVERY FOUR YEARS. HOW WILL YOU "LEAP FORWARD" OR CHALLENGE YOURSELF TODAY?

MARCH IS WOMEN'S HISTORY MONTH.
WRITE ABOUT A STRONG WOMAN IN YOUR LIFE.
HOW WILL YOU CELEBRATE HER?

WOMEN'S
HISTORY
MONTH

MARCH

2

WHAT DOES IT MEAN TO BE
BRAVE?

AS A SUPER HERO, CAPTAIN MARVEL HAS TO DEAL WITH A LOT OF STRESSFUL SITUATIONS. HOW DO YOU WORK THROUGH THE STRESSFUL THINGS IN YOUR LIFE?

MARCH

4

"I myself have never been able to find out precisely what feminism is: I only know that people call me a feminist whenever I express sentiments that differentiate me from a doormat."

REBECCA WEST, JOURNALIST AND AUTHOR

WHAT DOES "FEMINISM" MEAN TO YOU?

**WHO IS YOUR FAVORITE SUPER HERO,
AND WHAT MAKES THEM SPECIAL?**

MARCH

6

THERE ARE LOTS OF TOYS, MOVIES, AND ACTIVITIES
OUT THERE THAT PEOPLE SAY ARE
"JUST FOR BOYS" OR "ONLY FOR GIRLS."
WRITE ABOUT SOMETHING YOU LIKE THAT MOST
PEOPLE WOULD SAY SHOULD BE ENJOYED
BY SOMEBODY OF ANOTHER GENDER.

WRITE DOWN YOUR FAVORITE FAMILY RECIPE AND EXPLAIN WHY IT'S AN IMPORTANT PART OF WHO YOU ARE.

8

WHAT DOES
"ACTING COURAGEOUSLY"
MEAN TO YOU?

WHEN WAS THE LAST TIME YOU FELT POWERFUL?
WRITE ABOUT IT HERE.

**CAPTAIN MARVEL CONSTANTLY PUSHES HERSELF
TO BECOME A STRONGER AND SMARTER FIGHTER.
WRITE ABOUT A TIME YOU HAD TO WORK HARD
IN ORDER TO GET BETTER.**

"Courage is not simply one of the virtues, but the form of every virtue at the testing point."

C. S. LEWIS, AUTHOR OF *THE CHRONICLES OF NARNIA*

MARCH

11

HAVE YOU EVER FELT LIKE YOUR BELIEFS WERE TESTED? HOW DID YOU STAND UP FOR WHAT YOU BELIEVED?

MARCH

12

**WHEN WAS THE LAST TIME
SOMEONE MADE YOU FEEL
ACCEPTED OR INCLUDED?**

CREATE A MOTIVATIONAL PLAYLIST THAT WILL
ENCOURAGE YOU TO TAKE ON THE WORLD.

MARCH

13

MARCH

14

ADMITTING YOU NEED HELP WITH SOMETHING
TAKES A LOT OF COURAGE.
WRITE A LIST OF REASONS WHY ASKING FOR HELP
IS ONE OF THE BRAVEST THINGS YOU CAN DO.

WHEN WAS THE LAST TIME
YOU WERE PROUD
OF YOURSELF?

MARCH

15

WHAT MAKES SOMEONE
STRONG?

BEING A HERO ISN'T JUST ABOUT HAVING POWERS, IT'S ABOUT TRYING YOUR BEST TO DO THE RIGHT THING. WRITE ABOUT A TIME WHEN YOU HAD TO WORK HARD TO DO WHAT WAS RIGHT.

MARCH

18

OF THE 50 UNITED STATES, ONLY 26
HAVE ELECTED A FEMALE GOVERNOR.
WHY DO YOU THINK THIS IS?

WHEN WAS THE LAST TIME YOU WERE
BRAVE?

MARCH

20

WHO ARE THE FIRST THREE PEOPLE THAT COME
TO MIND WHEN YOU THINK OF THE WORD "LEADER"?
WHAT CHARACTERISTICS DO THEY SHARE
THAT YOU CAN EMULATE?

MANY SUPER HEROES HAVE NAMES THAT ARE RELATED TO THEIR POWERS OR HOW THEY HELP PEOPLE. WHAT WOULD YOUR SUPER HERO NAME BE?

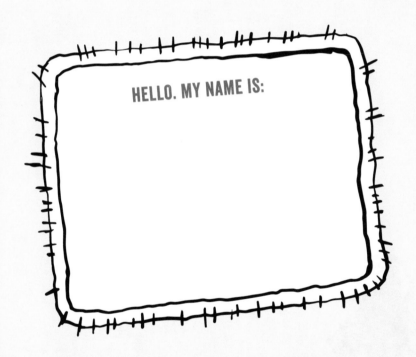

HELLO. MY NAME IS:

WRITE ABOUT THE LAST BOOK YOU READ
THAT MADE YOU FEEL STRONG OR EMPOWERED.

DESCRIBE YOUR BIGGEST FEMALE ROLE MODEL.
WHAT INSPIRES YOU ABOUT HER?

MARCH

24

"Life success is becoming the person
you want to be."

IRENE RINALDI, ARTIST

WHAT KIND OF PERSON DO YOU WANT TO BE?

AS A MEMBER OF STARFORCE,
CAPTAIN MARVEL MUST LEAD THE KREE
AND OTHER AIRMEN DURING SPACE FLIGHT.
WHAT TEAM DO YOU HOPE TO LEAD ONE DAY?

MARCH

25

MARCH
26

WHAT PIECE OF ADVICE WOULD YOU GIVE TO KIDS WHO ARE YOUNGER THAN YOU?

**CAPTAIN MARVEL WILL RISK EVERYTHING
TO FIGHT FOR THE PEOPLE SHE LOVES.
WHOM IN YOUR LIFE WOULD YOU RISK
EVERYTHING FOR, AND WHY?**

MARCH

28

WHAT ORGANIZATIONS OR CLUBS
ARE YOU A PART OF AT YOUR SCHOOL?
HOW ARE THEY HELPING OTHER PEOPLE
IN YOUR SCHOOL OR COMMUNITY?

**OUR DIFFERENCES ARE WHAT MAKE
US INTERESTING AND SPECIAL.
WRITE ABOUT A FEATURE, QUALITY, OR PERSONALITY
TRAIT YOU HAVE THAT IS DIFFERENT
FROM EVERYONE ELSE'S.**

MARCH

29

MARCH

30

CAPTAIN MARVEL WEARS A DISTINCTIVE UNIFORM THAT
MAKES HER LOOK FIERCE AND STRONG.
DRAW AN OUTFIT THAT EMBODIES YOUR IDENTITY
AND MAKES YOU FEEL CONFIDENT.

WHAT WOULD YOU DO IF YOU KNEW
YOU COULDN'T FAIL?

APRIL

1

TODAY IS APRIL FOOL'S DAY.
HOW WILL YOU MAKE SOMEONE LAUGH TODAY?

APRIL
FOOL'S
DAY

WRITE A POSITIVE LETTER TO YOUR BODY THANKING IT FOR ALL THAT IT DOES.

APRIL

3

**WHAT HELPS YOU TO BE
BRAVE?**

**LIST THREE THINGS YOU'RE REALLY
GOOD AT THAT MOST PEOPLE DON'T KNOW.**

5

"My mother told me to be a lady. And for her, that meant be your own person, be independent."

RUTH BADER GINSBURG, SUPREME COURT JUSTICE

WHAT HAVE YOU BEEN TOLD BEING A LADY MEANS?
DO YOU AGREE WITH THAT EXPLANATION OR NOT?

**BEING A SUPER HERO MEANS BEING STRONG
ENOUGH TO TALK ABOUT YOUR FEELINGS.
WHEN WAS THE LAST TIME YOU OPENED UP
TO SOMEONE YOU COULD TRUST?**

1

WHAT IS THE MOST IMPORTANT PIECE OF ADVICE YOU'VE EVER BEEN GIVEN?

WHAT ARE SOME WAYS THAT YOU CAN
BE MORE CONFIDENT?

9

WRITE ABOUT SOMETHING THAT'S EASY FOR YOU
THAT MIGHT BE HARDER FOR OTHERS.
HOW CAN YOU USE YOUR SKILLS TO HELP SOMEONE ELSE?

FINISH THIS SENTENCE:
"I FEEL STRONG WHEN I _____ ."

HOW DO YOU KEEP GOING WHEN SOMETHING YOU'RE WORKING ON GETS HARD?

**MAKE A LIST OF FIVE THINGS YOU'VE ALWAYS
WANTED TO DO BUT WERE TOO SCARED TO TRY.**

APRIL

13

**WRITE ABOUT A TIME YOU
STOOD UP TO A BULLY.**

IT'S EASY TO GET UPSET WHEN THINGS DON'T TURN OUT HOW WE WANT THEM TO. WHAT ARE SOME POSITIVE WAYS YOU CAN EXPRESS FRUSTRATION OR DISAPPOINTMENT?

APRIL

14

APRIL

15

"I hope I'll see in my lifetime a growing realization that we are one world."

DR. HELEN RODRIGUEZ TRIAS, WOMEN'S RIGHTS ACTIVIST

MAKE A LIST OF REASONS WHY PEOPLE'S DIFFERENCES ARE EXCITING AND IMPORTANT.

WHAT IS THE DIFFERENCE BETWEEN HELPING SOMEONE DO SOMETHING AND DOING IT FOR THEM?

16

APRIL

17

"We need to reshape our own perception of how we view ourselves. We have to step up as women and take the lead."

BEYONCÉ, PERFORMING ARTIST

HOW WILL YOU STEP UP AND LEAD TODAY?

SOMETIMES IT TAKES COURAGE JUST TO BE TRUE TO YOURSELF. HAVE YOU OR SOMEONE YOU KNOW EVER HAD TO BE BRAVE JUST BY BEING THEMSELVES?

APRIL

19

MAKE A LIST OF THREE THINGS THAT MAKE YOU NERVOUS OR UNCOMFORTABLE. WHAT CAN YOU LEARN FROM THEM?

IF YOU AND YOUR FRIEND WERE A SUPER HERO TEAM, WHAT WOULD YOUR LOGO LOOK LIKE? DRAW IT HERE.

APRIL

21

SOMETIMES THE MOST IMPORTANT LESSONS ARE THE ONES
THAT ARE THE MOST CHALLENGING TO LEARN.
WRITE ABOUT A TIME YOU LEARNED A DIFFICULT LESSON
THAT YOU WERE ULTIMATELY GRATEFUL FOR.

**DO YOU FEEL LIKE TODAY'S LEADERS ARE LISTENING
TO ORDINARY PEOPLE? WHY OR WHY NOT?
IF NOT, WHAT CAN YOU DO
TO MAKE YOUR VOICE HEARD?**

23

WRITE A LETTER TO ONE OF YOUR FLAWS AND TALK ABOUT WHY YOU LOVE IT INSTEAD.

WHAT MARVEL SUPER HERO DO YOU
ASPIRE
TO BE LIKE AND WHY?

24

APRIL

25

**WRITE ABOUT SOMEONE IN YOUR LIFE
THAT YOU'RE PROUD OF.**

**BEING OUR TRUE SELVES TAKES A LOT OF COURAGE.
HOW WILL YOU BOLDLY BE YOURSELF TODAY?**

APRIL

27

**WRITE ABOUT SOMETHING YOU ACCOMPLISHED RECENTLY.
HOW WILL YOU CELEBRATE?**

**TODAY IS NATIONAL SUPER HERO DAY.
DO YOUR BEST TO HELP SOMEONE IN NEED,
AND WRITE ABOUT THE EXPERIENCE HERE.**

NATIONAL
SUPER HERO
DAY!

APRIL

29

"The most damaging phrase in the language is: 'We've always done it this way.'"

GRACE HOPPER, COMPUTER SCIENTIST

TODAY, DO SOMETHING IN A NEW WAY INSTEAD OF HOW IT'S ALWAYS BEEN DONE. WHAT WAS IT LIKE?

WRITE ABOUT SOMEONE THAT INSPIRES YOU TO BE A BETTER PERSON.

MAY

1

**WHAT DOES IT MEAN
TO TREAT SOMEONE WITH
RESPECT?**

**DRAW A PICTURE OF WHAT YOU
THINK A HERO LOOKS LIKE.**

MAY

3

WHEN WAS THE LAST TIME YOU FELT
INVINCIBLE?

"To make peace, one must be an uncompromising leader. To make peace, one must also embody compromise."

BENAZIR BHUTTO, FORMER PRIME MINISTER OF PAKISTAN

DO YOU AGREE THAT A GOOD LEADER MUST LEARN HOW TO COMPROMISE? WHY OR WHY NOT?

MAY

5

EVEN THOUGH BECOMING A PILOT WAS REALLY HARD, CAPTAIN MARVEL SUCCEEDED. WHAT IS ONE DIFFICULT THING YOU WANT TO ACHIEVE?

DO YOU SEE YOURSELF IN A POSITIVE LIGHT? WHY OR WHY NOT?

1

WRITE ABOUT SOMEONE WHO ALWAYS MAKES YOU FEEL GOOD ABOUT YOURSELF.

**SUPER HEROES REGULARLY HAVE TO SAVE THE WORLD
FROM DANGER. IF YOU WERE A SUPER HERO,
WHO OR WHAT WOULD YOUR NEMESIS BE?**

8

MAY

9

DO ONE THING TODAY THAT MAKES YOU
STEP OUT OF YOUR COMFORT ZONE.
WRITE ABOUT THE EXPERIENCE HERE.

LIST THREE THINGS YOU LIKE ABOUT YOURSELF AND ONE THING YOU'D LIKE TO IMPROVE.

MAY

DO YOU BELIEVE CONFIDENCE IS CONTAGIOUS? WHY OR WHY NOT?

MOTHER'S DAY IS CELEBRATED AROUND THIS TIME. WRITE ABOUT A TIME YOUR MOM OR PARENT WAS BRAVE.

MAY

13

WHAT IS THE STRONGEST SUPER-POWER?

MAKE A LIST OF THINGS THAT YOU THINK ARE SYNONYMOUS WITH "INNER BEAUTY." HOW MANY OF THEM ALSO DESCRIBE YOU?

14

**IMAGINE A POWERFUL WOMAN.
WHAT DOES SHE DO AND WHAT DOES SHE LOOK LIKE?
DRAW A PICTURE OF HER HERE.**

THE KREE WORSHIP A GOD KNOWN AS THE
"SUPREME INTELLIGENCE" WHO APPEARS IN
A DIFFERENT FORM FOR EACH KREE MEMBER.
WHAT WOULD THE SUPREME INTELLIGENCE
LOOK LIKE TO YOU?

MAY

16

MAY

17

WHAT MOTIVATES YOU WHEN YOU'RE STRUGGLING
TO COMPLETE A TASK OR FINISH A PROJECT?

**TODAY, START A CONVERSATION WITH SOMEONE
YOU'VE ALWAYS WANTED TO TALK TO.
WHAT DID YOU LEARN ABOUT THEM?**

MAY

18

MAY

19

CAPTAIN MARVEL HAS VIVID MEMORIES FROM HER PAST THAT SHE CAN'T EXPLAIN. WHAT IS YOUR MOST IMPORTANT MEMORY?

FILL IN THE BLANKS:
"I LIKE _____ ABOUT MYSELF
BECAUSE _____ ."

MAY

20

MAY

21

HOW DO YOU TAKE CARE OF YOURSELF
WHEN YOU'VE HAD A BAD DAY?

WHAT IS THE DIFFERENCE BETWEEN CONFIDENCE AND SHOWING OFF?

MAY

23

"Great things are done by a series of small things brought together."

VINCENT VAN GOGH, PAINTER

WHAT ARE SOME LITTLE THINGS YOU CAN DO TODAY TO MAKE A POSITIVE CHANGE IN THE WORLD?

CONFIDENCE IS ABOUT LEARNING HOW TO EMBRACE OUR FLAWS. WRITE ABOUT SOMETHING YOU LOVE TO DO EVEN THOUGH YOU AREN'T VERY GOOD AT IT.

MAY

25

WHAT WOULD YOU DO IF YOU HAD
UNLIMITED POWER?

**IF YOU HAD UNLIMITED POWERS,
WOULD YOU KEEP THEM TO YOURSELF
OR SHARE THEM WITH THE WORLD?**

26

MAY

27

ON MEMORIAL DAY, WE HONOR THE EVERYDAY HEROES
WHO HAVE PROTECTED OUR COUNTRY.
THIS WEEK, TALK TO A VETERAN ABOUT THEIR
EXPERIENCES AND WRITE ABOUT THEM HERE.

BEING BOLD CAN SOMETIMES MEAN FAILING SPECTACULARLY. WRITE ABOUT A TIME YOU MADE A HUGE MISTAKE.

MAY

29

**CAPTAIN MARVEL'S CHARISMA OFTEN
DRAWS OTHERS TOWARD HER.
WRITE ABOUT ONE OF YOUR QUALITIES THAT
YOU THINK PEOPLE ARE DRAWN TO.**

SINCE SHE WAS A KID, CAPTAIN MARVEL
HAS WANTED TO LEARN HOW TO FLY.
WHAT IS ONE SKILL YOU HAVE ALWAYS
WANTED TO LEARN?

MAY

30

WHAT MAKES SOMEONE
"POWERFUL"?

BEING BRAVE CAN ALSO MEAN ADMITTING WHEN YOU'RE WRONG ABOUT SOMETHING. WRITE ABOUT A TIME WHEN THIS HAPPENED.

JUNE

2

DOING SOMETHING YOU'VE NEVER DONE
BEFORE CAN BE SCARY.
WRITE ABOUT THE LAST TIME
YOU TRIED SOMETHING NEW.

WHEN IS IT WORTH TAKING A RISK?

WHAT DOES IT MEAN TO BE
A LEADER?

**SUPER HEROES FIGHT BAD GUYS WHILE
OTHER HEROES FUND-RAISE OR RECYCLE.
WHAT ARE SOME THINGS YOU CAN DO TO HELP OTHERS?**

JUNE

6

**WHAT'S YOUR MOST IRRATIONAL FEAR?
WHEN DID IT START AND HOW CAN YOU OVERCOME IT?**

DO YOU THINK IT'S OKAY TO MAKE ASSUMPTIONS ABOUT SOMEONE BASED ON THEIR APPEARANCE? WHY OR WHY NOT?

JUNE

8

"Girl hate is not hating someone who happens to be a girl, it's hating someone because we're told that, as girls, we should hate other girls who are as awesome as or more awesome than ourselves."

TAVI GEVINSON, FOUNDER OF *ROOKIE MAGAZINE*

MAKE A LIST OF ALL THE GIRLS AND WOMEN IN YOUR LIFE AND WRITE DOWN ONE AMAZING THING ABOUT THEM. VOW TO TELL EACH PERSON WHAT YOU WROTE ABOUT HER WHEN THEY LEAST EXPECT IT.

WRITE ABOUT THE MOST
DARING THING
YOU'VE EVER DONE.

JUNE

10

**IF YOU WERE PRESIDENT, WHAT WOULD BE THE
FIRST LAW YOU'D PROPOSE AND WHY?**

WHAT DOES
EQUALITY
MEAN TO YOU?

JUNE

12

WHO IS YOUR HERO?
WRITE A STORY THAT SHOWCASES
WHAT YOU MOST ADMIRE ABOUT THEM.

HAVE YOU EVER BEEN PEER-PRESSURED BY OTHERS? HOW DID YOU OVERCOME IT?

JUNE

14

TODAY IS FLAG DAY, WHEN THE UNITED STATES CELEBRATES THE BIRTH OF THE NATION'S FLAG. CREATE A FLAG FOR YOUR FAMILY OR FRIEND GROUP AND DRAW IT BELOW.

DO YOU THINK IT'S EASY TO STAND UP TO AUTHORITY? WHY OR WHY NOT?

JUNE

15

JUNE

16

FATHER'S DAY IS CELEBRATED AROUND THIS TIME.
MAKE A LIST OF WHAT INSPIRES YOU MOST ABOUT
YOUR FATHER OR PARENT.

THE KREE ARE A HIGHLY INTELLIGENT ALIEN RACE THAT ONLY SLIGHTLY RESEMBLE HUMANS. CREATE YOUR OWN ALIEN RACE, AND DRAW A PICTURE OF THEM BELOW.

JUNE

18

SET A TIMER FOR THREE MINUTES. WRITE FOR THAT
AMOUNT OF TIME—WITHOUT STOPPING!—ABOUT WHAT
"COURAGE" MEANS TO YOU.

IF YOU WERE A SUPER HERO, WOULD YOU WORK WITH A SIDEKICK OR BY YOURSELF?

JUNE

19

JUNE

20

**CHOOSE ONE POSITIVE THING YOU'VE DONE
THIS WEEK TO CELEBRATE.
HOW WILL YOU REWARD YOURSELF?**

**CREATE A MANTRA TO HELP YOU GET
THROUGH TOUGH DAYS.**

JUNE

21

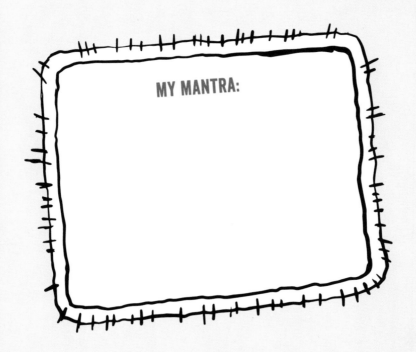

MY MANTRA:

22

FINISH THIS SENTENCE:
"I LIKE MYSELF WHEN _____."

**WRITE A LETTER TO YOUR FEARS.
SEE IF YOU CAN LEARN TO FACE THEM AS YOU WRITE.**

JUNE

24

WHEN WAS THE LAST TIME YOU GAVE SOMEONE ADVICE? WHAT DID YOU ADVISE THEM ON?

HOW CAN YOU HELP OTHER PEOPLE FEEL MORE CONFIDENT?

JUNE

26

WHAT IS THE
BRAVEST THING
YOU'VE EVER DONE?

DO YOU HAVE TROUBLE MAKING DECISIONS? WHAT CAN YOU DO TO HELP YOURSELF MAKE CHOICES MORE QUICKLY AND WITH CONFIDENCE?

JUNE

28

HOW DO YOU KNOW WHEN YOU'VE
SUCCEEDED
AT SOMETHING?

DO YOU IDENTIFY AS A FEMINIST? WHY OR WHY NOT?

JUNE

30

"I learned that courage was not the absence of fear but triumph over it. The brave man is not he who does not feel afraid, but he who conquers that fear."

NELSON MANDELA, POLITICAL LEADER AND PHILANTHROPIST

WRITE ABOUT A TIME THAT YOU PUSHED YOURSELF TO DO SOMETHING EVEN THOUGH IT SCARED YOU.

A HAIKU IS A POEM THAT HAS THREE LINES.
THE FIRST LINE HAS FIVE SYLLABLES,
THE SECOND LINE HAS SEVEN,
AND THE LAST LINE HAS FIVE.
WRITE A HAIKU ABOUT SOMETHING
YOU LOVE ABOUT YOURSELF.

JULY

2

WRITE ABOUT A PERSON IN YOUR LIFE WHO MAKES YOU FEEL CONFIDENT.

**NO ONE CAN SUCCEED WITHOUT
THE SUPPORT OF OTHERS.
WHEN WAS THE LAST TIME
YOU FELT TRULY SUPPORTED?**

JULY
4

TODAY IS INDEPENDENCE DAY IN THE UNITED STATES. WRITE ABOUT WHAT "INDEPENDENCE" MEANS TO YOU.

FOURTH
OF
JULY

WRITE ABOUT A TIME IN HISTORY
WHEN PEOPLE HAD TO SHOW
COURAGE.

JULY

6

THERE ARE MANY JOBS WHERE THE MAJORITY OF THE WORKERS ARE MEN.
WHAT JOB OR TRADE WOULD YOU LIKE TO SEE MORE WOMEN WORKING IN AND WHY?

**WRITE A SHORT STORY ABOUT A GIRL
WHO HAS TO STAND UP FOR HERSELF.
DOES SHE SUCCEED?**

JULY

8

IN 1948, ESTHER MCGOWIN BLAKE ENLISTED
IN THE U.S. AIR FORCE ON THE FIRST MINUTE
OF THE FIRST DAY WOMEN WERE ALLOWED TO DO SO.
WHAT IS SOMETHING YOU WOULD LIKE TO BE
THE FIRST PERSON TO DO?

WHAT IS YOUR
GREATEST STRENGTH
AND WHY?

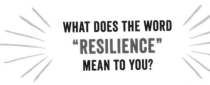

FINISH THIS SENTENCE:
"I FEEL HAPPIEST IN MY SKIN WHEN _____ ."

JULY

12

HAS THERE EVER BEEN A TIME WHEN YOU
DIDN'T FEEL GREAT ABOUT YOURSELF?
HOW DID YOU OVERCOME IT?

WRITE ABOUT A TIME SOMEONE DOUBTED YOU
AND YOU PROVED THEM WRONG.

JULY

14

MAKE A LIST OF ALL THE PEOPLE IN YOUR LIFE WHO APPRECIATE YOU.

NAME SOMETHING YOU HAVE A QUESTION ABOUT
BUT ARE TOO EMBARRASSED TO ASK.
HOW CAN YOU GET THE COURAGE TO ASK
SOMEONE ABOUT IT?

JULY

16

ARE YOU EVER TOO HARD ON YOURSELF?
LIST SOME WAYS YOU CAN EASE UP ON YOURSELF.

**DRAW FOUR COMIC BOOK PANELS THAT ILLUSTRATE
THE BEST THING THAT HAPPENED TO YOU THIS WEEK.**

JULY

18

IF YOU COULD MEET ANY INFLUENTIAL WOMAN, WHO WOULD IT BE AND WHY?

WHAT IS SOMETHING YOU NEED TO LET GO OF SO YOU CAN MOVE FORWARD?

20

CREATE A PLAYLIST THAT MAKES YOU FEEL STRONG.
WHAT SONGS WILL YOU CHOOSE? WHAT WILL
YOU DO WHILE LISTENING TO THEM?

HOW DO YOU FEEL WHEN SOMEONE COMPLIMENTS YOU?
HOW CAN YOU START COMPLIMENTING OTHERS
MORE OFTEN?

JULY

21

JULY

22

IF YOUR BEST FRIEND WAS BRAGGING ABOUT YOU, WHAT WOULD SHE SAY?

WRITE ABOUT A TIME YOU WERE STRUGGLING
AND HAD TO ASK FOR HELP.
WHAT DID YOU LEARN BY ASKING FOR SUPPORT?

JULY

24

FINISH THIS SENTENCE:
"I WILL ALWAYS _____ ."

TELLING THE TRUTH TAKES A LOT OF COURAGE.
HAS THERE EVER BEEN A TIME YOU HAD TO BE HONEST
WITH SOMEONE? WHAT WAS IT LIKE?

JULY

26

DON'T BE AFRAID OF YOUR FEELINGS!
TODAY, TELL SOMEONE YOU CARE ABOUT
HOW MUCH THEY MEAN TO YOU.

IF YOU HAD TO RESCUE ANY FICTIONAL WORLD FROM DESTRUCTION, WHICH ONE WOULD YOU CHOOSE AND WHY?

JULY

28

**WHAT DO YOU SEE WHEN YOU LOOK IN THE MIRROR?
WRITE ABOUT IT AND THEN
DRAW A PICTURE OF YOURSELF HERE.**

"This nation was founded on one principle above all else: the requirement that we stand up for what we believe, no matter the odds or the consequences. When the mob and the press and the whole world tell you to move, your job is to plant yourself like a tree beside the river of truth and tell the whole world—'No, **YOU** move.' "

CAPTAIN AMERICA

WRITE ABOUT A TIME YOU HAD TO FIGHT FOR WHAT YOU BELIEVE IN.

JULY

30

WRITE A LETTER TO YOUR GREATEST WEAKNESS.
HOW CAN YOU LEARN TO EMBRACE IT?

WHAT MAKES YOU FEEL SAFE OR SECURE?

JULY

31

AUGUST

1

PICK A FEMALE ARTIST TO LEARN MORE ABOUT.
HOW DOES HER WORK INSPIRE YOU?

WHAT MAKES YOU FEEL
ACCOMPLISHED?

CHOOSE TEN POSITIVE ADJECTIVES TO DESCRIBE YOURSELF, AND USE YOUR FAVORITE COLORS TO WRITE THEM!

WHY IS IT IMPORTANT TO
MAKE MISTAKES?

AUGUST

4

AUGUST

5

HOW DO YOU THINK OTHER PEOPLE PERCEIVE YOU?
IS IT SIMILAR TO HOW YOU SEE YOURSELF?

**SOMETIMES SUPER HEROES DON'T
GET NOTICED FOR THE GOOD WORK THEY DO.
DO YOU THINK IT'S IMPORTANT TO BE RECOGNIZED
FOR YOUR GOOD DEEDS? WHY OR WHY NOT?**

AUGUST

6

"The hardest challenge is to be yourself in a world where everyone is trying to make you be somebody else."

E. E. CUMMINGS, POET AND AUTHOR

HAVE YOU EVER FELT LIKE SOMEONE WANTED YOU TO BE LIKE SOMEONE ELSE?

WHAT IS ONE THING THAT YOU ALWAYS BRING WITH YOU FOR STRENGTH OR LUCK? DRAW A PICTURE OF IT HERE.

8

AUGUST

9

CAPTAIN MARVEL SOMETIMES HAS FLASHBACKS FROM HER PAST. IF YOU HAD THE OPPORTUNITY TO ERASE CERTAIN MEMORIES, WOULD YOU CHOOSE TO?

AUGUST
11

DOES BEING LOYAL MEAN GOING ALONG WITH SOMETHING YOU DISAGREE WITH? WHY OR WHY NOT?

**WHERE WE GROW UP PLAYS A BIG ROLE IN OUR IDENTITIES.
WRITE ABOUT WHAT YOUR HOUSE, YOUR CITY, OR
YOUR COUNTRY MEANS TO YOU.**

AUGUST

12

AUGUST

13

**HAVE YOU EVER HELPED A TOTAL STRANGER?
WHAT WAS IT LIKE?**

**IF YOU COULD REINVENT YOURSELF TODAY,
WHAT KIND OF PERSON WOULD YOU BE?
IF YOU WOULDN'T CHANGE A THING, WRITE ABOUT WHY!**

AUGUST

14

AUGUST 15

WHAT IS A CAUSE OR POLITICAL ISSUE YOU WOULD LIKE TO LEARN MORE ABOUT? RESEARCH THREE NEW FACTS ABOUT IT AND WRITE THEM DOWN HERE.

**MANY PEOPLE LOOK UP TO SUPER HEROES
SUCH AS CAPTAIN MARVEL.
WHO DO YOU LOOK UP TO?**

AUGUST

17

**HOW DO YOU CHEER YOURSELF UP
WHEN YOU'RE FEELING BLUE?**

WHO IN YOUR LIFE TEACHES YOU THE MEANING OF HARD WORK?

AUGUST

18

19

MANY GIRLS AROUND THE WORLD TODAY STILL
AREN'T ABLE TO MAKE CHOICES FOR THEMSELVES
ABOUT THEIR HEALTH OR EDUCATION.
WHAT CAN YOU DO TO HELP OTHER GIRLS NEAR AND FAR?
BRAINSTORM A LIST OF IDEAS AND VOW TO PUT
THREE INTO ACTION THIS MONTH.

"Don't try to comprehend with your mind. Your minds are very limited. Use your intuition."

MADELEINE L'ENGLE, AUTHOR

HAVE YOU EVER HAD A GUT FEELING ABOUT SOMEONE OR SOMETHING? DID YOU TRUST IT?

20

AUGUST

21

WRITE ABOUT A TIME YOU SHARED SOMETHING PERSONAL ABOUT YOURSELF WITH SOMEONE ELSE. HOW DID IT MAKE YOU FEEL?

THINK OF THREE POWERFUL WOMEN IN YOUR LIFE.
IF YOU COULD GIVE THEM SUPER-POWERS,
WHAT WOULD THEY BE AND WHY?

23

WHAT DOES
"RESPONSIBILITY"
MEAN TO YOU?

YOU HAVE BEEN TASKED WITH CREATING A NEW SUPER HERO FOR MARVEL STUDIOS. WHAT DO THEY LOOK LIKE? WHAT CAUSE(S) DO THEY FIGHT FOR OR WHOM DO THEY PROTECT?

AUGUST

24

AUGUST

25

**WHEN DO YOU THINK PEOPLE SEE
YOU AT YOUR BEST?**

**DO YOU BELIEVE YOU ARE WORTHY ENOUGH
TO PICK UP THOR'S HAMMER, MJÖLNIR?
WHY OR WHY NOT?**

AUGUST

27

**WRITE A LETTER TO YOUR YOUNGER SELF.
WHAT ADVICE OR WORDS OF WISDOM WOULD YOU GIVE?**

FINISH THIS SENTENCE:
"I LOVE THAT I CAN _____ ."

AUGUST

28

AUGUST

29

WHERE DO YOU THINK
CONFIDENCE
COMES FROM?

**HAVE YOU EVER FELT STUCK OR IN A RUT?
HOW DID YOU GET OUT OF IT?**

31

"The odd thing about these deep and personal connections of women is that they often ignore barriers of age, economics, worldly experience, race, culture—all the barriers that, in male or mixed society, had seemed so difficult to cross."

GLORIA STEINEM, JOURNALIST AND ACTIVIST

ARE YOU FRIENDS WITH SOMEONE WHO IS DIFFERENT FROM YOU? HOW HAVE YOUR DIFFERENCES STRENGTHENED YOUR FRIENDSHIP?

THE START OF SCHOOL CAN BE A STRESSFUL TIME. WRITE DOWN FIVE PHRASES OF ENCOURAGEMENT TO REFLECT ON WHEN SCHOOL GETS TOUGH.

SEPTEMBER

 1

 2

 3

 4

 5

SEPTEMBER

2

WHAT MAKES YOU FEEL
CARED FOR?

HAVE YOU EVER VOLUNTEERED OR FUND-RAISED
FOR AN ORGANIZATION? MAKE A LIST OF THREE
ORGANIZATIONS YOU CAN VOLUNTEER AT
IF YOU HAVEN'T ALREADY.

SEPTEMBER

4

WHAT ACADEMIC GOALS DO YOU WANT TO ACHIEVE THIS YEAR?

WHICH OF THE AVENGERS DO YOU THINK IS THE BRAVEST AND WHY?

SEPTEMBER

5

SEPTEMBER

6

LIST THREE VALUES THAT YOU LOOK FOR IN A FRIEND. WHY ARE THEY IMPORTANT?

IT CAN BE HARD TO ADMIT WHEN WE DON'T KNOW SOMETHING. TODAY, RAISE YOUR HAND OR SPEAK OUT WHEN YOU ENCOUNTER SOMETHING YOU DON'T KNOW. WHAT DID YOU LEARN?

SEPTEMBER

7

SEPTEMBER

8

LIST FOUR FEMALE WRITERS WHOSE WORK YOU HAVEN'T READ BUT WOULD LIKE TO READ SOMEDAY.

HOW DO YOU FEEL WHEN SOMEONE RECOGNIZES YOUR ACCOMPLISHMENTS?

SEPTEMBER

10

FINISH THIS SENTENCE:
"A STRONG PERSON IS SOMEONE WHO _____ ."

SEPTEMBER

12

**WHAT IS YOUR FAVORITE
MOTIVATIONAL QUOTE?**

FAVORITE MOTIVATIONAL QUOTE:

SUPER HEROES ARE CONSTANTLY GETTING HURT. WHEN WAS THE LAST TIME YOU WERE INJURED? WRITE THE STORY OF HOW IT HAPPENED.

SEPTEMBER

13

SEPTEMBER

14

CAPTAIN MARVEL HAS TO SACRIFICE HER REPUTATION AMONG THE KREE IN ORDER TO DISCOVER THE TRUTH ABOUT HER PAST. HAVE YOU EVER HAD TO SACRIFICE SOMETHING IMPORTANT FOR SOMETHING GREATER?

**WHAT MAKES YOU FEEL ENVIOUS?
WRITE ABOUT HOW YOU CAN CHANNEL YOUR ENVY
INTO GRATITUDE INSTEAD.**

SEPTEMBER

15

SEPTEMBER

16

**DO YOU FEEL MORE COMFORTABLE BEING
A LEADER OR A FOLLOWER?
WHAT ARE THE PROS AND CONS OF BOTH SIDES?**

"I know my value."

PEGGY CARTER, SSR AGENT AND S.H.I.E.L.D. FOUNDER

PEGGY CARTER MUST WORK HARDER THAN MOST PEOPLE TO SHOW EVERYONE WHAT SHE CAN DO. HAVE YOU EVER STRUGGLED TO PROVE YOURSELF?

17

SEPTEMBER

18

WRITE **FIVE AFFIRMATIVE STATEMENTS** ABOUT YOURSELF THAT START WITH "I AM," SUCH AS "I AM KIND" OR "I AM STRONG." THEN, TEAR OUT THIS PAGE AND TAPE IT INTO YOUR NOTEBOOK OR TO THE INSIDE OF YOUR LOCKER FOR WHEN YOU NEED A PICK-ME-UP.

I AM...

I AM...

I AM...

I AM...

I AM...

WHAT MAKES YOU FEEL ENERGIZED?
TAKE SOME TIME TO DO THAT THING TODAY.

20

**WRITE A POEM USING THE WORDS
"FEMALE" AND "POWER."**

CAPTAIN MARVEL SOMETIMES STRUGGLES TO GET ALONG
WITH OTHER MEMBERS OF THE STARFORCE TEAM.
HOW DO YOU WORK OUT DISAGREEMENTS
WITH YOUR FRIENDS?

SEPTEMBER

21

DO YOU THINK GIRLS EXPERIENCE PRESSURES THAT ARE DIFFERENT FROM THOSE EXPERIENCED BY BOYS? ARE THEY BETTER OR WORSE? WRITE DOWN YOUR THOUGHTS HERE.

WHO IS THE BRAVEST PERSON YOU KNOW?
WHY DO THEY DESERVE THAT TITLE?

SEPTEMBER

24

**TAKING CARE OF THE ENVIRONMENT IS JUST
AS IMPORTANT AS TAKING CARE OF OURSELVES.
WHAT ARE SOME WAYS YOU CAN CONTRIBUTE
TO HELPING THE PLANET?**

WHAT IS YOUR FAVORITE THING ABOUT YOUR BRAIN? IS IT YOUR VIVID DREAMS? YOUR ABILITY TO DO MATH IN YOUR HEAD? WRITE ABOUT IT HERE.

SEPTEMBER

26

WHAT DOES BEING
SUCCESSFUL
MEAN TO YOU?

WRITE ABOUT A TIME YOU WERE FEARLESS.

SEPTEMBER

28

HAS THERE EVER BEEN A TIME WHEN SOMEONE ELSE'S CONFIDENCE MADE YOU FEEL LESS CONFIDENT? HOW DID YOU WORK THROUGH IT?

**SOME PEOPLE THINK THAT BOYS
ARE STRONGER THAN GIRLS.
DO YOU THINK THAT'S TRUE? WHY OR WHY NOT?**

SEPTEMBER

29

SEPTEMBER

30

LIKE THE AVENGERS OR GUARDIANS OF THE GALAXY,
SOME FRIEND GROUPS HAVE A NAME.
DOES YOUR FRIEND GROUP HAVE ONE?
IF SO, DRAW A POSTER WITH THE NAME
OF YOUR SQUAD BELOW. IF NOT, CREATE ONE!

WRITE ABOUT SOMETHING YOU DID WELL RECENTLY. HOW DID IT FEEL?

OCTOBER

2

WHAT IS THE BEST WAY TO HELP SOMEONE WHO IS STRUGGLING IN CLASS?

OCTOBER

4

USE THIS PAGE TO WRITE A HAPPY NOTE TO YOURSELF.
TEAR IT OUT AND LEAVE IT SOMEWHERE IN YOUR ROOM
TO FIND WHEN YOU LEAST EXPECT IT.

**WHAT IS THE GREATEST COMPLIMENT
SOMEONE HAS EVER GIVEN YOU?**

OCTOBER

5

OCTOBER

6

WHAT DOES IT MEAN TO LOVE SOMEONE "UNCONDITIONALLY"?
DO YOU FEEL THAT WAY ABOUT YOURSELF?

WRITE DOWN THREE THINGS YOU ACCOMPLISHED TODAY, NO MATTER HOW SMALL.

OCTOBER

8

FINISH THIS SENTENCE:
"I BELIEVE I CAN _____ ."

WHY DO YOU THINK IT'S IMPORTANT TO HAVE HIGH SELF-ESTEEM?

BEING EMPOWERED MEANS NOT BEING AFRAID
TO USE YOUR VOICE. **TODAY, STATE YOUR OPINION
ON AN ISSUE YOU CARE ABOUT. HOW DID IT FEEL?**

TODAY IS NATIONAL COMING OUT DAY.
DO YOU KNOW SOMEONE WHO IS PART
OF THE LGBTQ COMMUNITY?
HOW CAN YOU SUPPORT THEM TODAY?

OCTOBER

11

NATIONAL
COMING
OUT DAY

OCTOBER

12

FROM CAPTAIN AMERICA'S MOTORCYCLE TO BLACK PANTHER'S CUSTOMIZED SEDAN, EVERY HERO NEEDS A GETAWAY VEHICLE. USE THIS PAGE TO DESIGN YOUR OWN CAR OR SPACESHIP. THEN, WITH THE HELP OF A PARENT OR GROWN-UP, BUILD IT USING RECYCLED MATERIALS FROM AROUND THE HOUSE.

**HAVE YOU EVER HAD TO RESCUE SOMEONE
OR INTERVENE IN A DIFFICULT SITUATION?
WHAT WAS IT LIKE?**

14

WHAT DO YOU WISH THE ADULTS IN YOUR LIFE UNDERSTOOD ABOUT BEING A KID?

"You have brains in your head, you have feet in your shoes. You can steer yourself any direction you choose. . . . And YOU are the one who'll decide where to go . . ."

DR. SEUSS, AUTHOR

YOU'RE IN CONTROL OF YOUR OWN DESTINY! WHERE DO YOU WANT TO GO TODAY? WHAT ABOUT NEXT WEEK? NEXT YEAR? OR FIVE YEARS FROM NOW?

OCTOBER

16

**HAVE YOU EVER HAD TO DO SOMETHING
YOU DIDN'T AGREE WITH?
HOW DID YOU HANDLE IT?**

SET ASIDE 30 MINUTES TODAY TO DO SOMETHING THAT MAKES YOU FEEL GOOD. IS IT EXTRA READING TIME OR A WORKOUT CLASS? WRITE IT DOWN HERE.

OCTOBER

18

**WRITE A STORY ABOUT
A PRINCESS WHO RESCUES A PRINCE
INSTEAD OF THE OTHER WAY AROUND.**

DO YOU KNOW SOMEONE WHO IS HAVING A HARD TIME?
HOW CAN YOU SHOW THEM THAT YOU CARE ABOUT THEM?
IF YOU YOURSELF ARE STRUGGLING, MAKE A PROMISE TO
YOURSELF THAT YOU'LL TELL SOMEONE TODAY.

OCTOBER

19

WHAT DO YOU LIKE ABOUT YOUR GENDER?
WRITE ABOUT IT HERE.

DRAW A PICTURE OF YOUR BRAIN WITH ALL YOUR
THOUGHTS, DREAMS, AND WORRIES INSIDE.
IS MOST OF YOUR BRAIN DEVOTED TO NEGATIVE
THOUGHTS AND WORRIES? WHAT CAN YOU DO
TO THINK MORE POSITIVELY INSTEAD?

OCTOBER

21

OCTOBER

22

WHO IS YOUR FAVORITE FEMALE POLITICAL FIGURE? HOW DOES SHE INSPIRE YOU?

WHAT DOES THE WORD "PERFECTION" MEAN TO YOU? DO YOU ASSOCIATE IT WITH NEGATIVE OR POSITIVE THINKING?

OCTOBER

23

MAKE A LIST OF THE QUALITIES THAT YOU
ASSOCIATE WITH BEING A GOOD PERSON.
HOW MANY OF THESE QUALITIES DESCRIBE YOU?

IN 1977, NASA LAUNCHED THE VOYAGER SPACE PROBES, WHICH WERE LOADED WITH AN ARRAY OF SOUNDS SO THAT IF ANY EXTRATERRESTRIALS EVER FOUND THE CRAFT, THEY WOULD KNOW WHAT LIFE WAS LIKE ON EARTH. IF YOU HAD TO PUT TOGETHER A CAPSULE OF ITEMS THAT DESCRIBE YOU, WHAT WOULD YOU CHOOSE AND WHY?

OCTOBER

25

OCTOBER

26

DO YOU PERFORM THE SAME ROUTINE EVERY DAY?
TODAY, STEP OUTSIDE THE BOX AND TRY DOING SOMETHING
A NEW WAY! TAKE ANOTHER ROUTE TO SCHOOL,
TRY WRITING WITH THE OPPOSITE HAND, OR FOLD
YOUR SHIRTS DIFFERENTLY. HOW DID IT FEEL?

WE CAN ALWAYS LEARN SOMETHING FROM OTHERS,
EVEN PEOPLE WE DISAGREE WITH. TODAY, TALK TO SOMEONE
WHO YOU KNOW HAS A DIFFERENT OPINION THAN YOU ON
A CERTAIN ISSUE. WHAT WAS IT LIKE?

OCTOBER

27

OCTOBER

28

DO YOU THINK IT'S BETTER TO HIDE YOUR FEELINGS
OR TO BE OPEN ABOUT THEM? WHY?

DO YOU THINK COURAGE AND BRAVERY ARE THE SAME THING?

OCTOBER

30

WHAT IS THE
SCARIEST
THING THAT HAS
EVER HAPPENED TO YOU?

**TODAY IS HALLOWEEN.
HAVE YOU EVER DRESSED UP AS A SUPER HERO?
WHAT WOULD YOUR COSTUME LOOK LIKE?
DRAW IT HERE.**

31

NOVEMBER

1

THERE ARE A LOT OF NEGATIVE PORTRAYALS OF WOMEN
AND GIRLS IN MOVIES AND MAGAZINES.
FILL THIS PAGE WITH PICTURES OF THE KINDS OF WOMEN
YOU WANT TO SEE IN THE WORLD.

"The woman who can create her own job is the woman who will win fame and fortune."

AMELIA EARHART, AVIATION PIONEER

—————

IS THERE A JOB YOU'D LIKE TO HAVE
THAT DOESN'T EXIST YET?
CREATE IT! DESCRIBE IT HERE.

WHAT MAKES SOMEONE A GOOD ROLE MODEL?

**CAPTAIN MARVEL'S KREE NAME IS VEERS
WHILE HER NAME ON EARTH IS CAROL DANVERS.
WHAT IS THE STORY OR ORIGIN OF YOUR NAME?**

NOVEMBER

5

**WRITE ABOUT SOMETHING
THAT MADE YOU SMILE TODAY.**

WHAT QUALITY OR PERSONALITY TRAIT DO YOU WISH YOU HAD? HOW CAN YOU ACQUIRE IT?

6

NOVEMBER

1

CHOOSE A WOMAN IN HISTORY WHO DID
SOMETHING COURAGEOUS.
WHAT CAN YOU LEARN FROM HER?

NOVEMBER

9

HOW DO YOU STAY POSITIVE DURING TOUGH TIMES? WRITE DOWN THREE WAYS YOU CAN STAY UPBEAT WHEN THINGS GO WRONG.

THINK ABOUT YOUR BAD HABITS.
WHAT CAN YOU DO TO BREAK THEM?

NOVEMBER

10

NOVEMBER

11

TODAY IS VETERAN'S DAY.
HOW WILL YOU HONOR YOUR NATION'S HEROES?

HAPPY
VETERAN'S
DAY

DRAW A PICTURE OF YOURSELF FEELING
CONFIDENT.

12

NOVEMBER 13

**WRITE SIX QUESTIONS YOU WOULD
LIKE TO ASK A REAL-LIFE HERO.**

WHAT DOES
SELF-LOVE
MEAN TO YOU?

NOVEMBER

14

NOVEMBER

15

CAN SAYING NOTHING BE AS IMPACTFUL
AS DOING SOMETHING?
WRITE DOWN EXAMPLES OF SITUATIONS WHERE STAYING
SILENT OR SPEAKING OUT WOULD MAKE A DIFFERENCE.

"It's very scary to allow the world to see you."

BRIE LARSON, ACTOR

WHAT CAN YOU DO TO STAY TRUE TO YOURSELF WHEN BEING AUTHENTIC IS HARD?

17

**WHAT MAKES SOMEONE
A SUPER HERO?**

WHAT DOES THE WORD "REBEL" MEAN TO YOU? WOULD YOU DEFINE YOURSELF AS A REBEL?

NOVEMBER

18

NOVEMBER

19

WHAT WOULD YOU DO IF YOU WEREN'T AFRAID?
MAKE A LIST AND TRY TO TACKLE ONE
OF THE ITEMS THIS WEEK.

FINISH THIS SENTENCE:
"I LOVE MY BODY BECAUSE _____."

NOVEMBER

20

NOVEMBER

21

**DRAW FIVE THINGS THAT MAKE YOU
HAPPY.**

**ARE YOU A GOOD ROLE MODEL?
HOW CAN YOU BE ONE FOR SOMEONE IN YOUR LIFE?**

WITH SO MANY RESPONSIBILITIES TO UPHOLD, IT'S EASY TO GET OVERWHELMED. PRACTICE SAYING NO TO SOMETHING THIS WEEK. DO YOU HAVE MORE TIME AND ENERGY AS A RESULT?

NOVEMBER

24

NOVEMBER

25

WHAT IS SOMETHING YOU WISH OTHER PEOPLE KNEW ABOUT YOU?

TODAY, SHOW THREE PEOPLE ONLINE
THAT YOU CARE ABOUT THEM.
CAN YOU COMMENT ON SOMEONE'S STATUS
ABOUT WINNING A GAME AND CONGRATULATE THEM?
OR LIKE THEIR SELFIE AND TELL THEM HOW COOL
THEY LOOK? DO IT!

NOVEMBER

27

THINK ABOUT AN ACTIVITY OR TASK THAT YOU OFTEN
DO WITH SOMEONE ELSE'S HELP.
IF IT'S SAFE TO DO SO, CAN YOU DO IT
BY YOURSELF? TRY IT!

THANKSGIVING IS A TIME TO SHOW GRATITUDE
FOR ALL THE POSITIVE THINGS IN YOUR LIFE.
MAKE A LIST OF PEOPLE IN YOUR LIFE WHOM YOU'RE
GRATEFUL FOR. THEN, TELL THEM!

NOVEMBER

28

NOVEMBER

**WHO IS YOUR BIGGEST SUPPORTER?
WRITE THEM A LETTER AND THANK THEM.**

29

"I love bossy women. I could be around them all day. To me, bossy is not a pejorative term at all. It means somebody's engaged and ambitious and doesn't mind leading."

AMY POEHLER, ACTOR

HAS ANYONE EVER DESCRIBED YOU AS "BOSSY"? HOW DID YOU RESPOND?

WHAT WOULD HAPPEN IF KIDS RULED THE WORLD? WHAT WOULD CHANGE AND WHAT WOULD STAY THE SAME?

HAVE YOU EVER WORKED WITH SOMEONE FROM
A DIFFERENT SCHOOL, NEIGHBORHOOD, BACKGROUND,
OR ETHNICITY? WHAT DID YOU LEARN FROM THEM?
WHAT DO YOU THINK THEY LEARNED FROM YOU?

3

FILL IN THE BLANK:
"I'M AFRAID PEOPLE WON'T ACCEPT ME
IF THEY KNEW _____ ."
NOW PICTURE A LOVED ONE SAYING THAT TO YOU.
WOULDN'T YOU STILL LOVE AND ACCEPT THEM? BE BRAVE
AND TELL ONE OF THOSE PEOPLE THAT THING TODAY.

"Have courage and be kind."

CINDERELLA

HOW CAN YOU BE KIND AND COURAGEOUS TODAY?

4

5

WRITE DOWN THREE POSITIVE THINGS THAT HAPPENED TO YOU TODAY.

**WHEN WAS THE LAST TIME
SOMEONE THANKED YOU FOR SOMETHING?
WHAT DID YOU DO FOR THEM?**

DECEMBER

6

WHAT'S ONE THING YOU LOOK FORWARD TO EVERY DAY? WRITE A POEM ABOUT IT HERE.

WHY DO YOU THINK
FEMALE SUPER HEROES
ARE IMPORTANT?

8

DECEMBER

9

**ANXIETY IS BEING STUCK IN THE PAST
AND AFRAID OF THE FUTURE.
WHAT ARE SOME WAYS YOU CAN BE LESS ANXIOUS?**

HOW DO YOU
RISE ABOVE
NEGATIVITY?

DECEMBER

10

DECEMBER

11

FINISH THIS SENTENCE:
"I'M DETERMINED TO _____ ."

WRITE DOWN ALL THE WORDS THAT YOU THINK OF WHEN YOU THINK OF "BRAVERY." HOW MANY OF THESE WORDS WOULD DESCRIBE YOU?

DECEMBER

HELP SOMEONE STEP OUT OF THEIR COMFORT ZONE TODAY.
ENCOURAGE THEM TO WEAR SOMETHING DIFFERENT OR TRY
SOMETHING NEW. WRITE ABOUT IT HERE.

13

**WRITE DOWN ALL THE THINGS THAT ARE STRESSING
YOU OUT. NOW CROSS OFF THE THINGS YOU
CAN'T CONTROL. FROM NOW ON,
VOW TO WORRY ABOUT ONLY WHAT YOU CAN CHANGE.**

DECEMBER

15

IF YOU WERE A SUPER HERO,
WHAT WOULD YOUR SYMBOL BE?
DRAW IT HERE.

WHAT MAKES YOU FEEL
TRULY ALIVE?

DECEMBER

17

THINK ABOUT A TIME WHEN YOU WANTED TO STOP
OR THOUGHT YOU COULDN'T KEEP GOING.
HOW DID YOU PERSEVERE?

WHAT MAKES YOU FEEL
POWERFUL?

DECEMBER

19

HAVE YOU EVER FELT INTIMIDATED BY SOMEONE ELSE'S SUCCESS? HOW CAN YOU OVERCOME IT AND CHANNEL IT INTO SOMETHING POSITIVE?

TAKE A LOOK AT YOUR BUCKET LIST.
(IF YOU DON'T HAVE ONE, MAKE ONE!)
ARE ALL OF THE THINGS ON IT EASILY ATTAINABLE?
BE BOLD AND ADD SOME PIE-IN-THE-SKY ITEMS
OR THINGS THAT YOU MIGHT NOT OTHERWISE TRY.

DECEMBER

20

DECEMBER

21

IF YOUR LIFE WERE A MOVIE, WOULD YOU BE THE STAR
OR THE SUPPORTING CHARACTER?
IF THE LATTER, HOW CAN YOU LEAD
A MORE AFFIRMATIVE LIFE?

WHEN YOUR FAMILY STARTS TO GATHER TO CELEBRATE THE HOLIDAYS, **THINK ABOUT THE WAYS YOU CAN CONTRIBUTE IN A NEW WAY. THE MORE UNEXPECTED THE BETTER! WRITE ABOUT WHAT YOU LEARNED HERE.**

DECEMBER

23

WHAT IS YOUR
GREATEST JOY?

"Remember, George: no man is a failure who has friends."

CLARENCE, *IT'S A WONDERFUL LIFE*

MAKE A LIST OF ALL THE WAYS YOUR LIFE HAS POSITIVELY IMPACTED YOUR FRIENDS AND FAMILY.
REMEMBER—YOU MATTER!

DECEMBER

TODAY IS CHRISTMAS DAY, BUT THERE ARE
MANY HOLIDAYS THAT HAPPEN THIS TIME OF YEAR,
LIKE BOXING DAY, HANUKKAH, KWANZAA, AND YULE.
PICK A HOLIDAY THAT YOU DON'T ALREADY CELEBRATE
TO LEARN MORE ABOUT.

**THINK ABOUT YOUR HAPPIEST MEMORY.
CAN YOU CREATE A HAPPY MEMORY FOR SOMEONE ELSE?
TRY IT TODAY AND WRITE ABOUT HOW IT MADE YOU FEEL.**

27

FINISH THIS SENTENCE:
"I CAN DO ANYTHING BECAUSE _____ ."

**WHAT WAS YOUR GREATEST CHALLENGE THIS YEAR?
HOW DID YOU FACE IT?**

28

DECEMBER

29

THINK ABOUT ALL THE AMAZING THINGS THAT HAPPENED
THIS YEAR. WRITE DOWN THE ONE THAT IMPACTED
YOU THE MOST AND WHAT YOU LEARNED FROM IT.

MAKE A LIST OF ALL THE THINGS YOU LIKE ABOUT
YOURSELF. THEN, LOOK BACK AT THE LISTS
YOU MADE EARLIER THIS YEAR.
IS TODAY'S LIST LONGER? IT SHOULD BE!

DECEMBER

30

DECEMBER

31

CHOOSE YOUR FAVORITE COLORED PENS, CRAYONS,
OR MARKERS AND WRITE DOWN SOME WORDS
OF AFFIRMATION THAT YOU CAN REFLECT ON AS
YOU CONFIDENTLY MOVE INTO NEXT YEAR.
NEED A PUSH? HOW ABOUT:

BE BOLD. BE BRAVE. BE YOU.